The story of *The Pied Piper* has been passed down for generations. There are many versions of the story. The following tale is a retelling of the original version. While the story has been cut for length and level, the basic elements of the classic tale remain.

Long ago, millions of rats took over the town of Hamelin, Germany.

The Pied Piper

Retold by Eric Blair
Illustrated by Ben Peterson

www.raintreepublishers.co.uk
Visit our website to find out
more information about
Raintree books.

To order:
☎ Phone 0845 6044371
🖹 Fax +44 (0) 1865 312263
✉ Email myorders@raintreepublishers.co.uk

Customers from outside the UK please telephone +44 1865 312262

Raintree is an imprint of Capstone Global Library Limited,
a company incorporated in England and Wales having its registered office at 7 Pilgrim
Street, London, EC4V 6LB
– Registered company number: 6695582

First published by © Stone Arch Books in 2011
First published in the United Kingdom
in paperback in 2012
The moral rights of the proprietor have been asserted.

Art Director: Bob Lentz
Designer: Hilary Wacholz
Production Specialist: Michelle Biedschied
Editor: Catherine Veitch
Originated by Capstone Global Library Ltd
Printed and bound in China by Leo Paper Products Ltd

ISBN 978 1 406 23020 8
15 14 13 12 11
10 9 8 7 6 5 4 3 2 1

British Library Cataloguing in Publication Data
A full catalogue record for this book is available
from the British Library.

At first, the rats stayed under the streets.
But soon they became bolder.

The rats began to go into people's homes.

The people were afraid.

7

Before long, rats were everywhere.
At night, they made so much noise
that no one could sleep.

The mayor of the town called a meeting.

Suddenly, there was a knock at the door.
A stranger walked in.

The stranger was dressed in a funny coat.
He had a silver pipe around his neck.

"I understand that your town has a rat problem," said the stranger.

"It does," said the mayor.

"For a fee, I will get rid of the rats," said the stranger.

13

"If you can get rid of the rats, one thousand gold coins will be yours," the mayor said.

"Deal," said the stranger.

That night, the stranger stepped into the
street. He began to play his pipe.

The rats came running.

They poured into the streets.

The stranger kept playing his silver pipe.

19

Then he marched towards the bridge.
When the stranger reached the middle
of the bridge, he raised his arm.

"Hippity-hop!" he cried.

All of the rats jumped into the river.
Soon, the king of the rats appeared.

The stranger asked, "Is that all of you?"

"Yes," the king rat said.

With that, the king rat threw himself from the bridge.

The next morning, the stranger found the mayor. "All of the rats are gone," he said. "It's time for you to pay me."

The mayor said, "We cannot pay you. We have no gold coins. The rats have destroyed our town."

The stranger became angry. Without a word, he stepped into the street. He began to play his pipe.

Children poured into the street.

The stranger marched out of town, playing his silver pipe as he went.

All of the children danced after him. When the stranger reached the mountain, it opened up.

The stranger and the children went inside. They were never seen again.